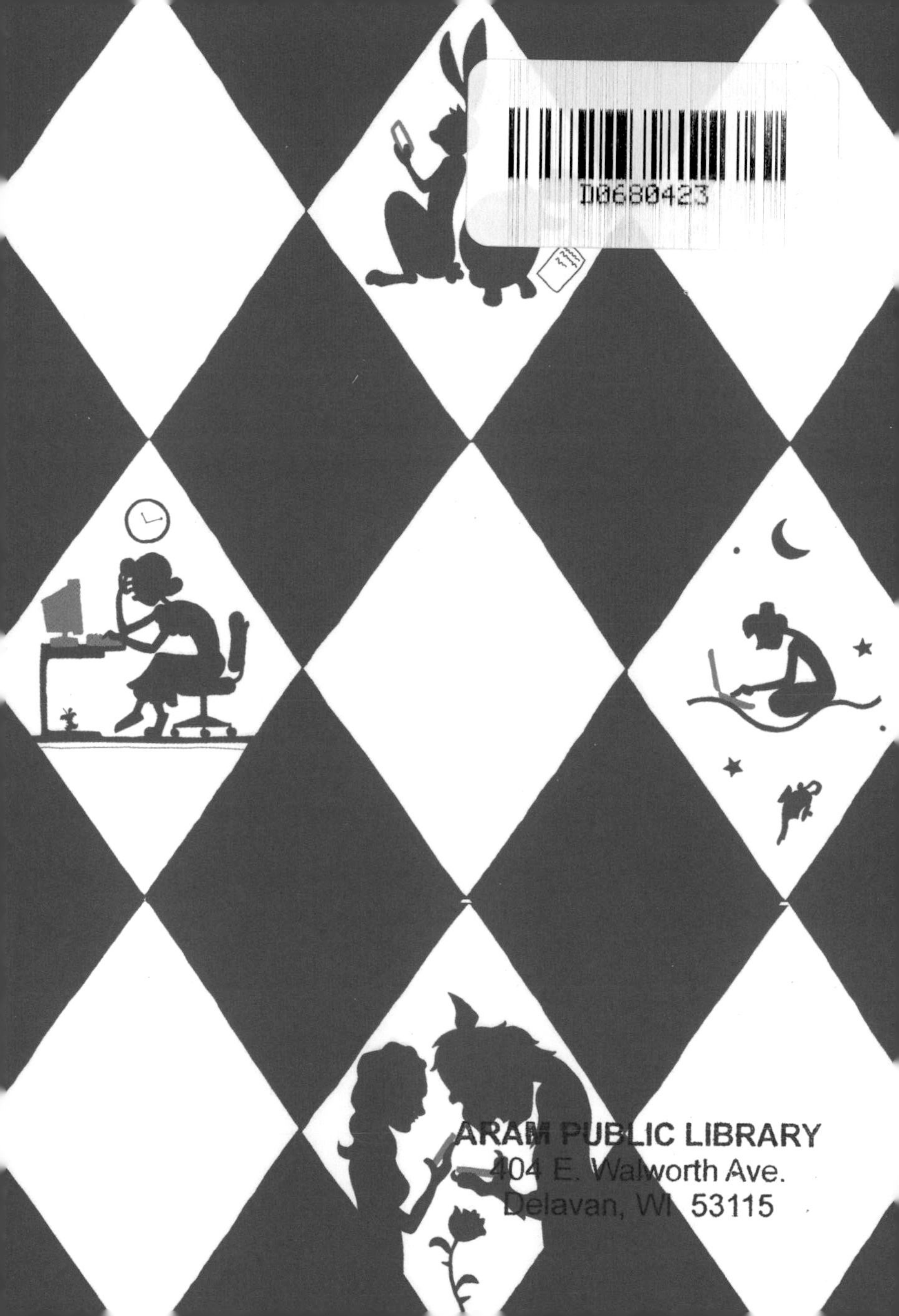

PENGUIN BOOKS

ALICE IN tumblr-LAND

AND OTHER FAIRY TALES FOR A NEW GENERATION

TIM MANLEY

PENGUIN BOOKS
Published by the Penguin Group
Penguin Group (USA) LLC
375 Hudson Street
New York, New York 10014

USA | Canada | UK | Ireland | Australia | New Zealand | India | South Africa | China
penguin.com
A Penguin Random House Company

First published in Penguin Books 2013

Some of the contents of this book appeared in different form on the author's blog, *Fairy Tales for
Twenty Somethings*.

LIBRARY OF CONGRESS CATALOGING-IN-PUBLICATION DATA
Manley, Tim.
Alice in tumblr-land : and other fairy tales for a new generation / Tim Manley.
pages cm
ISBN 978-0-14-312479-5
1. Fairy tales—Humor. 2. Parodies. I. Title.
PN6231.F285M36 2013
818'.602—dc23
2013031128

Printed in the United States of America
10 9 8 7 6 5 4 3 2 1

Set in Bodoni
Designed by Spring Hoteling

A few years had passed since Snow White and the Prince rode off toward their happily-ever-after, and things were, you know, they were fine.

Okay, so instead of going to bed with the Prince at night, Snow White found herself looking online at photos of Ryan Gosling, remembering the days when she'd felt for the Prince the same complex desire she now felt for Ryan. Like she wanted to simultaneously tear his clothes off and introduce him to her parents.

But the Prince loves me, Snow White thought. *And if I were with Ryan Gosling, he'd be hotter than me, and that wouldn't be cool at all.*

Beauty and the Beast had been dating for a while now, and Beauty knew it was time for the Beast to meet her friends. But she was a little nervous. All her friends had these superhot boyfriends who worked in finance or modeled for J.Crew or whatever. The Beast was, well, the Beast liked to play Xbox in his underwear. And he was *really* into his fantasy football team.

Beauty loved the Beast for who he was, she really did, but her friends were shallow and judgmental.

"Maybe you should get some new friends," Siri advised.

The Ugly Duckling still felt gross compared with everyone else. But then she got Instagram, and there's this one filter that makes her look awesome.

lice drank her tea and scanned the
news online. Even she had begun
to believe that what she'd "seen"
down the rabbit hole was just a figment
of her imagination. She'd since majored
in neuroscience; the human brain was
fascinating!

Peter Pan was up to something big. He'd been gone for days on what was likely some amazing new adventure, and when he finally returned home he looked like he'd been through his craziest battle yet.

"What mischief did you get into this time?" asked Tinker Bell.

"I've just been flying around, doing some thinking," said Peter. "All my friends are getting engaged, and some are having kids. I don't even have a steady job."

Rapunzel chopped off all her hair, and everyone was loving her new profile picture.

But then she was like, *Wait, did everyone hate my long hair and they just weren't telling me?*

After the whole wolf incident, the ideological differences among the Three Little Pigs only got stronger.

The First Little Pig went into the arts,

the Second Little Pig got a stable desk job,

and the Third Little Pig became a Republican.

9

Little Red Riding Hood decided to walk home from her grandmother's house because she didn't want to waste money on a cab.

But soon she was being stalked by a creepy wolf. He cornered her in the entryway to her apartment and started unzipping his pants, but then she was like, "Oh *hell* no," and kneed him in the balls and shot him in the face with pepper spray.

The next day she borrowed money from her mother and moved to a safer neighborhood.

*C*inderella divorced the Prince pretty quickly—no, he wasn't secretly gay, just kind of a prick—and moved back in with her stepmother.

As a symbolic gesture, she vowed not to wear glass slippers, or any slippers, ever again. From here on out, all Crocs, all the time.

Robin Hood sat on a stump, questioning his line of work. Sure, it helped on the local level, but what was he really doing to promote equality on a national level? Or a global level?

After thinking for a while, he determined that even though the work he did was very small, there was a ripple effect, so it was still a valuable endeavor. Plus, it got him a lot of girls.

15

The Hare got a high-powered job in the tech industry straight out of college. He was known for never sitting down at work and always chugging energy drinks. He invented a new app every day at lunch, though many of them were about sandwiches.

The Tortoise traveled the country by train just looking out the window and thinking. It didn't bother him that the Hare was out there making the big bucks. He was doing his own thing, something quieter, more spiritual.

The Tortoise's travel memoir got published, and the *New York Times* gave it a glowing review. The Tortoise posted on Facebook about how humbled he was by all this success, and he remembered his old rival the Hare and thought, *I knew I'd outshine that fucker in the end.*

After Arthur pulled the sword from the stone but before he became king, he went on a cross-country road trip/vision quest. He went to Burning Man, stayed in the mountains of Montana for a few weeks, and learned to build a cigar-box guitar from some guy on the street in New Orleans.

When he arrived home in Camelot, a wiser man, a man with true insight, he thought, *That shit was awesome.*

18 minutes ago via mobile

Lancelot: sweet pic bro

Guinevere: plank that mountain!

The Little Mermaid was now a human, but sometimes she still felt out of place. She didn't get the cultural references people made—and her hips swayed like crazy.

She tried her best to blend in, and she never spoke.

But at a party one night she overheard a group of elegantly dressed women discussing an episode of *Hoarders* about a woman who collected forks, and the Little Mermaid just had to jump in on that one.

"That's a very unusual accent you have," one of the women said to her. "Where are you from?"

Her past haunted her. She could never escape who she used to be.

21

Sleeping Beauty didn't get out of bed until noon, or even later. Instead she curled up in her blanket, wallowing in her depression and checking Facebook from her phone.

Then she came across a post from this prince she used to date about how sad he was, how there was a "darkness" that made him feel "like nobody could ever understand" how he felt.

"Is there anyone else who gets this way?" he asked.

Sleeping Beauty felt a sense of relief wash over her, a little bit of joy, and thought, *At least I'm not sad enough to write about it on Facebook.*

Peter Pan knew it was time to grow up, get serious, and work toward something substantial. So after hours of contemplation and soul-searching, he started a blog of funny anecdotes from his life. The Lost Boys read it, and they thought that shit was hilarious.

lice was amazed at the wonder of her life. Her rent was reasonable, she'd just discovered Greek yogurt, *and* she had the password to her friend's Netflix account.

She never thought of the past. Why should she?

But then the Cheshire Cat posted some photos from an old disposable camera online—of the White Rabbit with long hair, of the night they all stayed up till dawn just talking with the flowers—and God, it just brought her right back.

laddin had really screwed things up with Jasmine this time. Even the Genie thought he'd acted like "a total dickhead."

After what felt like 1,001 nights, he decided to win her back, to show her how he'd grown up, that now he was the man she'd always wanted him to be. He wanted to show her how brave he was, how he wasn't scared of emotions anymore, how he could even, one day, be a father to their children.

So he texted her, "hey, whats up?"

*C*inderella dreamed of being a photographer. But her stepmother had always told her she would amount to nothing, and at some point Cinderella had started believing her. It felt like the *truth*, even though a voice inside her pleaded that it wasn't.

One night she pulled out a Post-it and wrote a message to herself that she stuck on the wall above her desk: *You are in control of your own future. You are capable of amazing things.*

Then she added another one below that: *And fuck anyone who says otherwise.*

it's Thumb Boo Boo-lina!

Thumbelina never got much bigger, but she did get her own reality TV show, so that was cool.

Puss wore boots so that he would gain more respect, but everywhere he went people just said, "Omigod, look at that adorable kitty in boots!"

Beauty felt like she and the Beast were getting closer every day. They were totally in tune with each other; they really *understood* each other.

But then she accidentally stumbled on some weird porn sites he'd left open, and honestly, was *that* what he was interested in doing with her? Because, *hell* no.

Pinocchio e-mailed his professor and said, "I've had a family emergency and need one more day to work on my final paper."

The Frog Prince knew that all he needed to do was kiss a girl and he'd be turned back into a human. So he went to the bar and pulled off his signature move: standing in the corner praying that someone would approach him.

Hansel and Gretel got shitty jobs folding the boxes of gingerbread house kits.

Hansel thought of their grandfather, who'd gained dignity from his lifetime of work. But *this* work seemed so dehumanizing.

Hansel didn't know what to say about it; Gretel was the one who was good with words: "This blows."

J ack kept climbing beanstalks,
but none ever got him as high
as that first one.

Chicken Little feared the sky was falling.

She also feared losing her job, getting told off by her best friend, and going to the gynecologist.

Snow White didn't like Mondays, so she sang a song to get her through: "Just whistle while you work, and cheerfully together we can—" *Oh my God, how have only two minutes gone by? Somebody kill me now. I want to die.*

Arthur moved into a railroad-style apartment outside of Camelot with his buddy Lancelot. Arthur got a job at Applebee's, and Lancelot got one at Starbucks. They didn't care about their "careers." They just wanted to *live*.

Robin Hood was walking through the woods with Little John and wanted to tell him what was going through his head, but they were the same things he'd been stressing about since they were teenagers, and he thought he should really be over them by now . . .

They kept walking silently, the trees going by, the day going by.

Then it hit Robin Hood: *Is this how you get old? You slowly just stop talking about things?*

꙰

Sleeping Beauty kept turning off her alarm and falling back to sleep, so she decided to move her phone to the other side of the room, this way she'd be forced to get out of bed to turn it off. But then she just woke up lying on the floor halfway across the room.

Peter Pan's blog was a hit, but he knew that in today's market he'd need a multiple-platform approach to connecting with colleagues and branding himself, so he started a Twitter account.

For his first tweet he wrote: "Productive day w/ @LostBoys. Kicked Hook into crocodile's mouth AGAIN. #bangarang"

L ittle Red Riding Hood checked out the bougie bar in her new neighborhood, but even there she kept getting approached by wolves. She held her drink close to her and politely rebuffed them.

"Are you okay?" asked the gallant huntsman who approached her next.

"Ugh," she said, rolling her eyes. "Can't a girl just go out for a drink and be left alone?"

*A*lice found herself in a magical world she'd only dreamed about: Tumblr-land.

And there were so many marvelous sites! In ten minutes she'd researched the history of the Eiffel Tower, donated twenty dollars to a Kickstarter for a not-entirely-comprehensible art project, and learned, most important, never ever to go on Chatroulette again.

The Ugly Duckling read obscure works of literature in other languages and listened to indie music even the guys at the record store had never heard of.

If I'm not going to be prettier than anyone, the Ugly Duckling thought, *then I'm at least going to be better than them.*

The Frog Prince still needed that true-love kiss in order to turn back into a human, so he went to the park with a sign that said "Free Hugs" and figured he'd pull a switcheroo at the last second.

But this was, uh, not the best strategy.

After college, the Three Billy Goats Gruff moved to Brooklyn and started an indie rock band.

*A*rthur was driving home from Applebee's one night. Tired, cranky, his clothes smelling like dishwater and buffalo wings, he told himself, *I can't keep living like this. Tonight is the night I clean my apartment and make a to-do list. Tonight is the night I get my shit together.*

But before Arthur even had the chance to bust out the Swiffer, Lancelot showed him the page on Reddit where people post photos of themselves naked. What?! How did he not know about this?!

A laddin wanted to prove his love for Jasmine in one grand romantic gesture, so he texted her an Emoji heart.

Jasmine was a religious woman. She tossed aside the phone and knelt down to pray, seeking answers to the unanswerable questions.

"Why, Allah?" she said quietly. "Why do I always fall for such jackweeds?"

ansel and Gretel's boss was this sweet old lady who dressed all in black, cackled, and ate only candy corn.

But one day Hansel and Gretel had to use their boss's computer for a second, and they were horrified by what popped up.

Witch porn. Old ladies in cloaks bending over steamy cauldrons. And their boss with a broom disappearing into her—

"My eyes!" cried Hansel.

The Little Mermaid never knew what to say when somebody cracked a joke making fun of merpeople. Should she tell them she was offended? But it would require so much explanation. And nobody would believe the part about the octopus witch.

Wendy had kids right when she got back from Neverland, and then she was too fucking tired to do anything else.

It was spring, so Rapunzel took her new hair for a walk through the park, feeling like a woman reborn with the breeze tickling her scalp.

The past is only as meaningful as we decide it is, she thought. *We can become someone new, let ourselves be whoever we dream, and no one can tie us to who we used to be . . .*

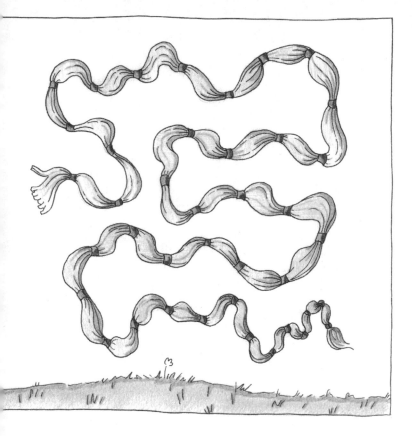

Then she ran into that douche she used to let climb up her hair at night.

"Oh my God—Rapunzel?!"

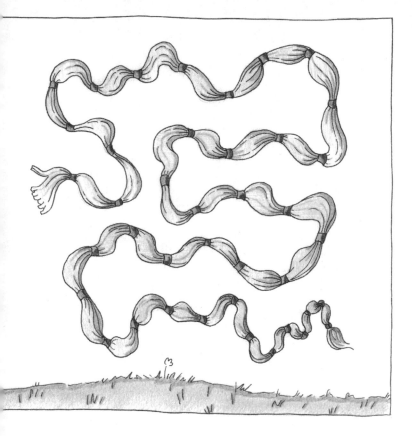

Alice was stuck in a small room in Tumblr-land with a tiny door the only exit. She tried the password for it a few times, but couldn't get the right combination of uppercase and special characters. It gave her a hint question, but who could remember their childhood best friend's cat's maiden name?

Peter Pan was all over the Internet now, racking up followers on social networking sites so new they hadn't even been acquired by Facebook yet.

But he found it had a weird effect on his psyche. Any time his brain was not 100 percent occupied, he felt the need to check the Internet. He'd checked his e-mail at the urinal at a bar, live-tweeted his phone call with Tiger Lily, even Instagrammed a photo of his laptop opened up to his Tumblr.

*C*inderella's day job was killing her, but she was too broke to quit. A part of her didn't care enough to quit anyway. What else would she do? It was stupid to think she could really be a photographer. Better to just accept her life and get used to it.

But another part of her wouldn't give up. As she lay awake listening to the mice scratch the walls, she closed her eyes and whispered,

"A dream is a wish your heart makes

When you're fast asleep . . .

I don't need everything to go right in my life, God;

I just wish I could care again.

Please. I just need to believe it's possible."

Mulan always preferred hanging out with the guys. She'd take a night of playing cards over an afternoon at the spa in a heartbeat. It kind of creeped her out, seeing other women naked; it always felt like their boobs were *looking* at her.

Yes, Beauty and the Beast were totally in tune with each other. And nowhere was this more evident than in the bedroom. Wow. Everything there was just . . . okay, so maybe recently things hadn't been *entirely* successful.

All Beauty's friends told her she and the Beast had to *communicate* more.

So they did. They started sexting.

G oldilocks kept taking fries off her friends' plates.

Then she'd be like, "Wait, does this have gluten in it?"

P inocchio told the interviewer, "Oh yeah, I have *tons* of restaurant experience."

Arthur didn't want all the responsibility that came with being king yet, so he just passed his days taking it easy and having a good time. He took Excalibur out pretty much only if he wanted to be really dramatic when cutting a sandwich.

Snow White was sitting down to a dinner the Prince had made for them, when she was suddenly overcome with this feeling of love for him. She wanted to know every part of him: his vulnerabilities, his fears, his dreams for the future—for *their* future.

Then the Prince said he was ready to have a baby, and Snow White was like, "I'm sorry, what?"

The Sheriff of Nottingham invited Robin Hood onto his TV show and said, "You've been giving to the poor for years, and they don't seem to be getting any less poor; don't you think it would be more effective to let the money trickle down from the job creators?"

Robin Hood replied, "Why don't we talk about something we can agree on?"

After what felt like an hour of silence, the Sheriff of Nottingham said, "So, do you like . . . ice cream?"

IS ROBIN HOOD THE PRINCE OF SOCIALISTS??

WOLF NEWS .COM

Sleeping Beauty was psyched it was Saturday. She had all this time to herself—anything was possible! Her friends had sent her a bunch of texts inviting her out. So, what would she do with her one wild and precious day?

Stay in her pj's and watch *30 Rock* in bed.

Yes, she thought, wrapping her Snuggie tighter, *this is the life.*

The Tortoise and the Hare Facebook-stalked each other.

The Tortoise looked at the Hare's Facebook photos of his swanky apartment and thought, *He may have material possessions, but does his work make him feel alive?* The Hare read the Tortoise's status updates and thought, *A writer in Brooklyn—how cliché.*

The truth was that a part of each of them longed for the other's life. How are you supposed to know if you've chosen the right path?

95

Peter Pan finally accomplished his dream.

"Found a way to never grow up?" asked Tinker Bell.

"Defeated Hook?" asked a Lost Boy.

"Even bigger," said Peter. "I made a meme that went viral."

*C*hicken Little feared that when people "liked" a photo she posted, they didn't *really* like it.

Wandering farther into Tumblr-land, Alice found her old friend the Caterpillar sitting atop a mushroom reading an e-book.

"Who are you?" the Caterpillar inquired, and Alice immediately had an existential crisis.

The Ugly Duckling liked to read at the bar, even though everyone else was there just to get laid. She was interested in more *important* things: art, the human condition, the fight to end poverty.

Then the guy she'd been eyeing all night left with this girl who was wearing some weird floral jeans or something. *It's always the manic pixie dream girl that gets the guy*, she thought. *Fuck you, manic pixie dream girl!*

Though Little Red Riding Hood harbored a growing disdain for anyone with a wang, she decided to give them one more shot, and signed up for OkCupid. Thousands of dateable suitors were just a click away!

But all she got were these creepy messages from wolves.

Well, that was disappointing, she thought, and went out and bought a vibrator.

0% Match
0% Friend
74% Enemy

BigTeeth

55/M/Straight+/Available
New York, NY

About | Photos Y'all Got Issues Tests

My self-summary

I am an honest, kind, loving gentleman.
Also still married.

What I'm doing with my life

Successful businessman.
Available flexible hours in the daytime.
Very generou$$$.

I'm really good at

;-)
(sex)

The first thing people usually notice about me

I'm wearing their grandmother's nightgown.
PS Are you into roleplay?

Arthur was loving his life of leisure, until one night when Merlin appeared at the door.

"Stop running away from your future," he said. "Accept responsibility for who you are capable of becoming."

Arthur was stunned.

"Damn," said Lancelot from the couch, exhaling a bong rip. "Shit just got real."

105

The Frog Prince wasn't having any luck finding that true-love kiss to turn him human, but he figured out a solution: He lowered his standards.

So he kissed a girl who was part troll. And a girl who wore those weird toe-shoes. And most frighteningly, he kissed a girl *from LA*.

The Little Mermaid was exhausted from trying to understand human society. How could corporations be legally considered people? And what the hell was dubstep?

Even the Lost Boys were starting to think Peter Pan's constantly being online was getting out of hand. Posting to Facebook from the toilet? Nobody should ever do that.

"It's no big deal," Peter told them, staring at the five open windows on his laptop, waiting for something to happen.

They printed out articles on the Internet's addictive nature, and tried to tempt him with a night of beer pong—"like the good old days!"—but he wasn't listening.

Finally they resorted to the only way they knew they could get through to him: They tweeted at him.

Sleeping Beauty's friends swore that her sleep habits were a sign of severe depression. And what was it she'd heard on TV? The first step to recovery is admitting you have a problem. Or was that only for addicts? Whatever. She decided to skip the first step and went straight to pouring herself a glass of wine.

I love this step, she thought.

ulan kind of dressed and acted like a guy, whatever that meant. Basically she *was* a guy, but a part of her didn't want to go all the way and start identifying as "he." She didn't think gender should have that much power. And what would she gain from transitioning to become a man?

Then one night at the movies she saw the line for the women's bathroom and was like, *Well . . .*

111

eeling a little lost in Tumblr-land, Alice thought to herself, *I'm quite sure I knew who I was when I was sitting in my kitchen, but right now I'm feeling a bit . . . wireless.*

Thankfully the Queen of Hearts had a surefire strategy she could follow to find herself.

Alice spent the next hour taking selfies in Photo Booth.

5246 photos

The Emperor got a new fedora, but his friends just thought it made him look like a tool.

J ack bought some beans at the market,
and whoa, they were *magical*.

Beauty and the Beast had become sext machines.

It was a little awkward at first—some of those terms should really have more delicate synonyms, and there was a bit of autocorrect confusion—but soon they were sending each other dirty messages like pros, complete with Snapchat crotch shots.

117

Peter Pan's constant connection to the Internet was making him feel less *present* in the real world, so he decided to get back to the things he did pre-Internet, to really live his life again.

That night, he watched TV for five hours straight.

It didn't get easier for Cinderella right away.

After a particularly tough day, she imagined what her mother would say to her if she were still here: *There are a few definitive moments when you can choose to either give up, or keep going, and in so doing prove the quality of your heart. This is one of those moments.*

So Cinderella decided to keep going. She also bought herself a fancy cupcake because it kind of just felt like the right thing to do.

Little Red Riding Hood's new battery-powered purchase was *certainly* worth the money—she'd named him Lil' Red—and she'd grown quite content with her man-free lifestyle.

And of course *that's* when she found a guy at the bar who wasn't some asshole wolf or douche bag huntsman. He was sweet, and she thought he was pretty funny, so she invited him back to her place. This was it! Finally!

But once in bed he was too nervous to, um, proceed forward.

Well, that was a bummer, she thought, and lit a cigarette.

The Boy Who Cried Wolf put on his résumé for the restaurant job that he was fluent in Spanish. But then he actually had to speak it with customers and—oh no, why did this old lady just slap him in the face?

Arthur was having dinner with Lancelot and the rest of the guys who would later become the Knights of the Round Table, talking about someone they used to know who was now famous. Or at least Internet-famous.

The knights all played it off like they didn't care, but Arthur lay awake that night thinking about it: *How do you know if you're the kind of person who will do amazing things, or if you're just the kind who will try and try and never get there?*

Robin Hood had successfully become a stable, functioning adult. While the rest of the Merry Men were panicking about what to do with their degrees in philosophy, Robin Hood was executing a strategically planned social media campaign for the welfare of the poor. Big kid stuff.

And he wasn't at all cracking under the pressure of growing up. It was only, like, once a month that he stayed up all night watching old Nicktoons and crying into a pack of Dunkaroos.

Though Sleeping Beauty would sleep the whole day away, she could never fall asleep at night.

At night she just sat refreshing her e-mail inbox over and over, each time seeming to prove just how much nobody in the world was thinking about her at that moment.

Except Obama. Obama e-mailed her, like, every ten minutes.

The Frog Prince was one lucky amphibian: He met the perfect girl while waiting in line at the comic book store. She had this bitchin' shaved-on-one-side haircut and a T-shirt of his favorite band, *and* she had a PETA pin, so he was like, *She's down.*

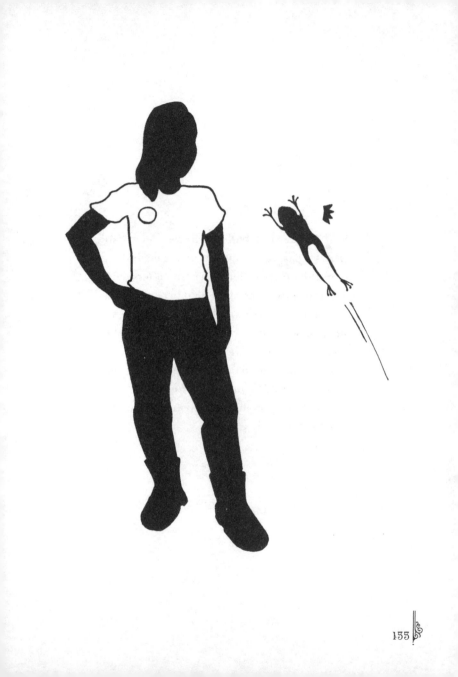

inker Bell had gotten over Peter Pan years ago, so it was no big deal when he invited her to tea one afternoon. But then he told her that he'd broken things off with Tiger Lily, and—it was crazy—all of a sudden she wanted him again. She could feel it like it was totally new.

Does this mean the feeling is real, or does it mean I'm just a fucking idiot? she thought to herself, and wished someone would clap for her.

MarchHare : a very merry unbirthday—
MadHatter : to who?
MarchHare : to me.
MadHatter : oh, you!
MarchHare : a very merry unbirthday to
          you.
MadHatter : who, me?
MarchHare : yes, you!
MadHatter : oh, me!

Arial   □□□ □ □□□   Send

A lice received an Evite from the Mad
Hatter to have tea with the March
Hare in an old-fashioned chat room.
How retro, thought Alice and typed
"24/F."

The Little Mermaid needed the company
of people who *understood* her, so she
went home to the ocean to visit her
father.

"So," he said when she arrived, "I guess you
think you're better than us now that you have
legs?"

As roommates, Arthur and Lancelot had gotten closer than ever, and somewhere along the line Arthur started having, um, well, sort of, *feelings*.

He wasn't asking too much! Just a friendly blow job . . . or maybe some brotherly mutual masturbation? It would be the same as always, except, you know, they'd have their pants down. No big deal!

Yes, tonight Arthur would bring it up.

But when he walked into their apartment, he found Lancelot and Guinevere naked together on the couch.

Well, he thought, *maybe not tonight, then.*

Beauty wasn't always called Beauty.

In high school she was "curvy," but the curves weren't in the places she'd wanted them. Kids called her Honey Bun. It would've been a cute nickname if it hadn't started when she got caught eating a ninety-nine cent honey bun behind the bleachers during gym class.

inderella had an idea for a project.

She wanted to photograph every single person who lived in her town—from the king to the guy who drove the horse and buggy—and do them as full-body standing portraits, like those old paintings of presidents. She would give everyone the honor they deserved. And she'd start with a photo of her stepmother.

The local bagel place put up prints of the first fifty portraits, and a few days later the town paper wrote a tiny thing about it.

Cinderella cut out the article and thought, *I feel like something big is about to happen. Like I'm in a Beyoncé song.*

*A*laddin knew the only way to win Jasmine back was to strike it rich again, but he had absolutely no idea how to do that.

Then he got an e-mail from a Nigerian prince who wanted to split an enormous inheritance with him, and he was like, *All he needs is my social security and bank account numbers? Well, that's easy!*

ansel and Gretel lost their jobs, and now they were living it up being funemployed! That is, they were sitting completely still, trying to not even think about spending money.

They didn't have anyone to turn to for financial support, because their parents had abandoned them in the woods when they were kids. They'd listened to a lot of Smashing Pumpkins as teenagers, but after all this time they'd calmed down.

"Sometimes," they had concluded, with a wisdom brought on by age and an open heart, "people are just fuckin' assholes."

P eter Pan was determined to grow up and become a man.

First step: Stop hashtagging words aloud.

HOW TO BE A MAN

1. stop hashtagging stuff out loud. it was only funny once.

2. get better jeans.

3. do P90X.

4. speak with confidence.

5. brew own beer.

THE END. MAN.

*A*lice, the Mad Hatter, and the March Hare drank tea and discussed whether the dreams they'd always held were really helping them to be *happy*. Capitalism, the Mad Hatter argued, postponed their contentedness into an ever-receding future because of its emphasis on always striving for more.

It was a thought-provoking conversation that ended with the kind of poignant silence that only old friends can share.

Then Alice thought, *Is this silence getting so long it's awkward? Well, now that I've thought about it, it's definitely awkward. Oh crap. What movies are out right now? Quick, Alice, think!*

The Ugly Duckling got a Facebook invite for her ten-year high school reunion.

Ugh, she thought. *I've had to look at these douche bags online all these years, and now I'm gonna have to see them in person?*

. . . I wonder what I should wear.

Rumpelstiltskin kidnapped another baby from some princess, and he was planning to do the whole creepy-dance-around-the-fire thing with it, but then he looked down and the baby had its toes in its mouth—its toes in its mouth! Ah! Frickin' adorable.

Everyone was loving Rapunzel's new short hair, but one unexpected consequence was that she kept getting hit on by women.

After, like, the tenth time, she wanted to say, "Is this still a thing—that only lesbians have short hair? Can't pretty much anyone have short hair now?" But then she was like, *Eh, YOLO*, and they made out.

C hicken Little spent the majority of her day googling things she was scared of.

She was scared she was pregnant.

She was scared she would never be able to get pregnant.

She was scared of Splenda, cockroaches, and IKEA (when it got crowded).

She was scared all her friends knew she wasn't interesting but weren't telling her because they felt bad for her.

Then one day she stopped herself and said, "No more googling every tiny fear!" Because she'd read this article about how laptops might cause cancer and—what!?— she was already at risk from always using the microwave.

Despite Prince Charming's repeated requests for children, Snow White couldn't understand why anyone would want a baby. Babies were like that really annoying girl at a party, but the party was all the time and the annoying girl kept grabbing at your breasts.

obin Hood was demoralized by the lack of support for his campaign for the poor. It suddenly felt naïve of him to have ever imagined real change was possible.

He decided to take a walk to clear his head, and he put on his headphones and played his favorite song.

Let the song put its arm over your shoulder and comfort you like a best friend would, he told himself. *And then go home and get back to work. You have a responsibility to other people now.*

*A*fter compulsively checking her inbox for twenty minutes, Sleeping Beauty found an e-mail, in her spam folder, from the Prince. It was a link to a YouTube video of some random girl singing the Tracy Chapman song "Fast Car."

The girl was good—not perfect, but good—but it was the vulnerability of the whole thing that got Sleeping Beauty. There was nothing "cool" about it; the girl was just quietly baring her heart, hoping someone would see. Sleeping Beauty clicked on a few other videos, all of regular people singing this one song they loved in the intimacy of their normal-looking bedrooms.

Her eyes teared up a little and she thought, *Ugh, I'm having* feelings.

*C*inderella was about to give up on her photography project when something magical happened: This massively popular art blog tweeted a link to her project, and she got thousands of visitors.

And after that, the real sign of success: Every guy she'd ever made out with sent her a message "just to say hi."

Fairy Godmother
@FairyG

arts & culture blog.
occasionally tweets food and/or
cats. bibbidi-bobbidi-boo.

Try as he might, Arthur just couldn't bring up his feelings with Lancelot. And he couldn't even look at the sword he'd pulled from the stone. It had become a symbol of his shortcomings.

It was from this dark place that Arthur embarked on the first of his legendary feats of bravery: He started a series of confessional YouTube videos.

Beauty had learned from thinspiration blogs that in order to maintain her name, she had to maintain her figure.

So when she was seventeen she stopped eating carbs. And fats. And anything larger than half the size of her palm. (But she had big hands!)

The Frog Prince asked the girl with the PETA pin to get a drink with him, and after a skeptical look, she agreed. And now he'd walked her home and they were outside her apartment, and she was leaning in toward him. This was it!

But he was going in for this openmouthed thing, and hers was just gonna be a little peck, so when their faces met, aw, it was . . . it was just a mess.

Little Red Riding Hood continued her masochistic tendencies with a string of terrible blind dates.

The first guy was obviously a wolf in women's clothing, which was disturbing on multiple levels.

The second guy really wanted her to keep her hood on through the meal, which seemed a little early in the night for weird fetishes.

And the last guy was *James Franco*. It was exciting for a minute, but then he started talking.

The Ugly Duckling arrived at her high school reunion bracing herself for the horror.

But surprisingly, her heart swelled when she saw everyone: all the ducks and squirrels from her youth, gathered at the same hall they'd used for their sweet sixteens. They were now adults. And though their lives were so different, their pasts kept them forever linked.

We're family, really, she thought. *Soldiers together in the war that is life.*

But then she saw Clarissa Anbowski and thought, *OMG, those are totally implants. What a ho-bag.*

S leeping Beauty did a WebMD search,
and yep, it looked like she should be
diagnosed with depression.
And syphilis? And a stroke!?

Jack became a minor celebrity after slaying the Giant, and he did all the late-night talk shows—except for Conan O'Brien, who was too tall for Jack's comfort.

The Gingerbread Man had gotten out of shape, and everything hurt. *I'm officially getting old*, he thought.

So he decided to start going on nightly jogs. Halfway through the first one he was feeling young and spry again, like back in his old high school track days, and he shouted proudly, "Run, run, run as fast as you can. You can't catch me, I'm the—AGH, MY KNEE! OH GOD, I TORE SOMETHING! THE PAIN IS EXCRUCIATING!"

The Little Mermaid finally broke up with Eric after he loudly joked to their friends that he'd "rescued" her from the ocean. That's when she knew he'd never seen her for who she really was.

But now she was alone, caught between two worlds and belonging to neither. What was someone supposed to do when they'd lost their sense of self and had no idea what to do with their lives?

The Little Mermaid applied to grad school.

P inocchio told the cop, "It's for my glaucoma!"

The Three Billy Goats Gruff started a movement called Occupy the Bridge, but everyone just seemed to think they were homeless.

Mulan did it: She got some surgery done up top and started taking testosterone. Hair started growing where there had been no hair before, like a second puberty—but without the awkward surprise during gym class.

The strangest part was the in-between phase, neither here nor there: This body right now— what would you call it?

Then one night, like magic, a transformation. He chose a new name, Ping. And the next day Ping took on his final challenge in his search for self: the line at the DMV.

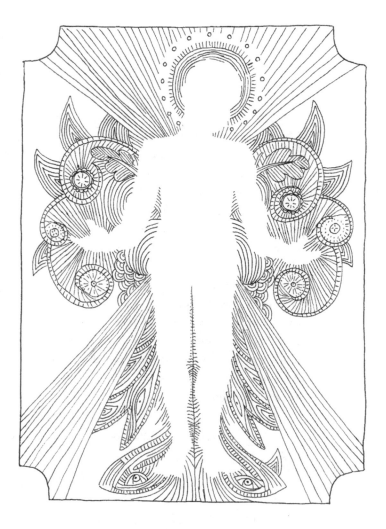

Robin Hood made some tweaks to his social networking campaign to provide welfare for the poor, and it took off immediately: Offices shared videos of their dance to the theme song, *SNL* parodied it, and college students brought it up in their essays on Plato's "Allegory of the Cave."

Only one problem: No one was actually donating money to the poor. They were only *sharing pictures* about doing it.

How am I supposed to get people to reach for their credit cards? he thought.

Then it hit him.

He sold T-shirts.

The Queen of Hearts threw a party to celebrate Alice's return. Alice was quite excited to have this opportunity to talk to her old friends and seek their help with her questions of identity, the past, and the future.

But then she got stuck in the corner talking with Tweedledee and Tweedledum the whole night, and they were totally shwasted. Where did they find black-market Four Lokos?!

Peter Pan knew he needed a real job, something he was passionate about, something that was *meaningful*. After months of searching, he hit it big: He got an unpaid internship with Captain Hook! His duties included answering the phones and . . . yeah, that was really it.

Snow White got the Dwarves together for some emergency wine and girl talk to weigh the pros and cons of the to-baby-or-not-to-baby situation.

On the downside, noted Bashful: walking in on your teenage son looking at porn.

On the plus side, said Sleepy: If she had a baby, she'd be allowed to leave a party whenever she wanted. *I really am fascinated with this conversation about the politics of "Gangnam Style," but sadly I must go, because, you know, the baby.*

But just before the debate got really heated, Doc sealed the deal for everyone—

Yes, Hansel and Gretel were a resilient duo, and refused to ask for help from anyone. They didn't need *money* anyway: They were freegans! They dumpster-dived for their food!

   . . . And, *completely* unrelated, they contracted hepatitis.

Rapunzel's family was supportive, but they had a few innocent questions now that she was dating a girl.

"Does this mean you're a lesbian?"

"Did you always know, or was it all of a sudden?"

"So do you get turned on looking at your own boobs? Like, if you looked at yourself in the mirror but not your face, would you be like, *niiiiiiiice?*"

That last one was from her brother.

Rapunzel explained that she wasn't trying to make some big *statement* with all these changes in her life. She was just doing what felt right.

"So," her brother said, "that's a no on the boobs?"

Beauty and the Beast got into a small discussion about the Beast's diet.

"I don't want to go on a juice cleanse," he said. "It makes me feel like I don't have teeth."

"It's healthy," she said.

"Why can't I just eat the bacon-wrapped bacon I invented?"

Beauty frowned.

"You're trying to change me," he said. "You're trying to make both of us people we aren't."

"I'm just trying to make us *better*," she said.

The Beast was a delicate flower at heart, so this hit him pretty hard. *Why is who we are not enough?*

Little Red Riding Hood was tired of all the dating BS; from now on she wanted to spend her time only on things that *mattered*. So she had lunch with her wise grandmother, the only person with real insight into what was significant in life.

"*Mi Roja*," her grandmother said, "why you not have a man?"

"Grandma—"

"One day you not be so pretty. Look at my *tetas*. Look! They hang like two animals, shot dead."

Little Red stared in horror.

"You *tetas* beautiful," her grandmother said. And added, as though pleading, "Have fun with them."

*C*inderella's moment of Internet fame was amazing, but all the magic disappeared when the clock struck midnight: Nobody was commenting on her status update anymore.

After finishing grad school, the Little Mermaid started a nonprofit to fight for the rights of mercitizens. She decided at that moment that she would never measure her success by financial gain, but instead only by how much good she contributed to the world. Money was irrelevant to her.

Later that day she got her first student loan bill.

Rumpelstiltskin was finding it hard to compete in this ever-changing world.

He'd successfully kidnapped a new baby, but it took only a few minutes for the princess to show up and guess his name. She'd google-image-searched "imp who steals babies."

And how did she know where to find him? He should've never "checked in" at "the secret hideout in the woods, exit 59, keep left."

207

Eventually Arthur told Lancelot about his feelings for him, but Lancelot didn't share his interest in getting high and then naked. Still, Arthur felt a sense of freedom rush through him, like he had nothing to lose because he was being completely honest about everything in his life.

So he confessed: "I've also been using your fancy shampoo."

"I thought so," said Lancelot, grinning.

They hugged it out like the best friends they would always be, and Arthur thought, *Please don't let me get a boner.*

When Captain Hook asked how Peter Pan's first day as an intern went for him, Peter told him he felt like the monotony had lightly pummeled his soul into submission.

"Ah, I remember that feeling," said Hook, a glint of nostalgia in his eyes. "That'll go away once you give up hope completely."

This will make great material for my blog, thought Peter Pan, and then he cried a little.

Pinocchio told his father, "I only need to move back home for a month, tops."

The White Rabbit was such a flake. Whenever he said to meet at eight, he'd never show up until at least eight thirty.

i'm late! i'm late! see you in a minute.
traffic is crazy! be there in 5.
a block away.
2 blocks.

Jasmine agreed to see Aladdin, just this once. They met at a coffee place they had no emotional attachments to and, after some conversation, Jasmine was struck with a revelation.

"It all comes down to listening," she said. "If we agreed to always *listen* to each other, then nothing can ever go wrong. It seems so easy now. How could it *not* work out?"

Aladdin didn't respond. He was texting under the table.

*C*hicken Little had always feared there was something wrong, even when she couldn't name what it was, like she'd been forgetting something she was supposed to be worried about—and that made her *really* worried.

But then she started going to therapy and realized all these things about her childhood and how they still affected her today, and she learned coping strategies.

She also started doing hot yoga.

L ittle Red Riding Hood ran into that guy who'd felt "a little shy, sorry," their first night in bed, and she invited him back to her place. Hey, she figured, at least she'd get felt up a little before he panicked and they just poured themselves drinks and talked about poetry.

But they must have grown closer even without having seen each other, because that night when they—all right, it didn't happen that night; it took another month before the guy felt totally safe with her, but *then*, wow, it really was . . . eh, it was good enough.

*A*lice got a little philosophical when she was drunk, so she went to her friend the Cheshire Cat to talk out her concerns about the direction of her life.

"Seems to me you're overthinking this whole thing," the Cheshire Cat advised. "I'd worry less about *who* you are, or *where* you're going, and just be it and go there. That's how I do it, anyway."

Then he hacked into her computer and e-mailed links for tail-enhancement pills to everyone in her contacts list.

free trial!
all natural!
no longer
causes tail
dysfunction!

225

Peter Pan officially disconnected from the Internet after an unfortunate incident involving an accidental "reply all" and some attached photos he'd intended just for Tiger Lily.

Goldilocks was always trying on her friends' clothes. Then she'd be like, "Oh, this is *way* too big for me."

After much deliberation, Snow White decided to become a mom, but with a few rules: The Prince would be a stay-at-home dad. And she would *not* be one of those mothers who posted photos of her kid on Facebook every day.

But then she got this really good shot in which her daughter didn't look *so much* like the baby from *The Curious Case of Benjamin Button*, and she was like, *Okay, just one.*

Like · Comment

 Doc: the fairest in the land!

 Grumpy: cute fuckin' kid.

Ping quickly got used to his new name, but his father kept slipping and calling him Mulan. It was fine, though. His father also called the Internet "AOL," so . . .

Cinderella kept the faith, and eventually her photo portraits of everyday people in her town were getting put up in a real gallery in the city.

She had one request: Keep the prices low. She wanted people who didn't collect art to be able to afford the pictures. Regular people hanging up photos of other regular people in their living rooms—there was something beautiful about that.

At the opening, Cinderella wore a dress she'd bought just for the occasion. She kept waiting for the crowd to reveal itself as a flash mob prank—for something to prove the secret truth that she was actually a failure—but it never happened.

You're just gonna have to face the facts, she told herself. *You're kind of a badass mofo.*

There was the story Rapunzel had expected for her life: a damsel in distress stuck in a tower, dreaming to be rescued. But then there was the one she'd made for herself: a bad bitch with a buzz cut, a hybrid car, and a hot girlfriend.

She preferred the one she'd made.

I choose what I take with me in life, and where I go with it, she said to herself in the bathroom mirror. *And I will bravely face the future, a fearless warrior completely undeterred by whatever is to—WAIT, am I getting crow's-feet?!*

Robin Hood and Little John wanted to have some intimate best friend time, so they sat near each other and shared links over Facebook.

"I feel older," Robin Hood messaged Little John, along with a link to a list of signs you were born in the nineties. "I know I've been saying that since we were, like, seventeen, but I feel older."

"Me too," typed Little John, and Robin Hood felt his heartbeat subside. He was relearning how to open up to his friend.

Then Little John giggled and messaged him a new link.

"Dude, your balls are totally showing in this picture."

The Prince and the Pauper unfriended each other because neither could stand the other's political status updates.

The Three Little Pigs each fared differently during the economic recession.

The First Little Pig lost his job,

the Second Little Pig lost his house,

and the Third Little Pig made millions in government bailouts.

S leeping Beauty met up with her old prince friend for coffee.

He spoke openly about some recent hardships in his life, somehow completely vulnerable without seeming needy or desperate—like he was *comfortable sharing his feelings*. Weird.

Then she talked: Her mother had been a quiet woman. It was looking at her one afternoon that put the thought in young Sleeping Beauty's mind that life was sad, and once in there it never left. She had been pricked by a cursed spindle, and it couldn't be undone.

"I hear ya," the Prince said, and with that little phrase, Sleeping Beauty felt something inside her begin to lift.

259

I t didn't happen after the first kiss.

   The Frog Prince and the PETA pin
   girl had been dating for weeks, maybe
months. They'd kissed; they'd done a lot
of really lovely fun things that definitely
counted as more than kissing, including
one or two things the girl suggested that the
Frog was like, "Yeah? Whatever you say!"

   But the fact remained: He was still a
frog . . .

. . . Still, he had this feeling inside. She was such a good person. He kept thinking of that phrase "heart of gold." And he knew that if he could find a way to stick with this girl for as long as possible, she'd make his life into something he'd only dreamed it could be. He just knew it.

Pinocchio's conscience finally broke down and told him, "You can't keep lying. It's obviously not working for you."

Pinocchio countered, "What if I put all my lies on Wikipedia? Would that make them true?"

After careful consideration, his conscience replied, "Only if you source them properly."

Pinocchio

From Wikipedia, the free encyclopedia

Pinocchio is a world-renowned basketball superstar,[1] Internet mogul,[2] and inventor of the roller coaster.[3]

Born and raised on the island from LOST,[4] he has collected every single Pokémon without even trying that hard.[5] He won the gold medal in 2004 for napping.[6] He definitely is not scared of penguins,[7] even though don't they have really shifty eyes??[8][9]

Pinocchio has dated Kim Kardashian[10] and Kanye West,[11] separately and together.[12][13][14] He has never made out with a JC Penney mannequin.[15] Who would do that??

Pinocchio wrote the song "Bridge over Troubled Water."[16]

ansel and Gretel found a box of photos and letters from when their family was still together. They passed them back and forth, quietly pointing out discoveries, each one a breadcrumb to who their parents really were.

"They were just young idiots," said Gretel, photo in hand.

"Like us," said Hansel.

And the two poured themselves some whiskey and stayed up late talking, pretending it wasn't a big deal that they were opening up to each other.

They were all each other had. They were brother and sister.

After the Pied Piper led the rats and children away from the village with his magic flute, he initiated his secret plan to steal the adults as well: He gave them each a GPS, but it always led them the wrong way.

The morning after her high school reunion, the Ugly Duckling saw that a friend had posted a bunch of photos from the reunion, and she thought, *Uh-oh, time for some good old-fashioned untagging.*

But hey! She didn't look terrible in them, and one of them she *loved*. A simple shot of her taken while she was talking to a friend. She couldn't remember what they'd been talking about, but she knew it had felt great. It was like she could actually be less guarded with this friend than with herself.

Something about the Ugly Duckling looked different in the picture. Around the eyes? She looked . . . she wouldn't use the word *beautiful*; she just looked *right*.

Beauty and the Beast had gradually grown distant. They didn't even ballroom-dance around the dining room anymore. And who could remember the last time the teapot had written a song about their love?

So when Beauty got a Facebook message from that guy who used to balance ten beer glasses on his biceps, she thought, *It could be nice at least to have a drink with him.*

Then the Beast ran into the room like an excited little kid, grabbed the remote, and said, "It's Shark Week!"

This man, Beauty thought, smiling, *this is the man for me.* And she closed her laptop.

When Arthur finally pulled Excalibur back out from under his bed, it was even more difficult than pulling it from the stone had been. The truth was that he faced his future with a mix of courage and desperation; he did it because it was his only choice.

(Merlin said he was going to stop paying Arthur's rent.)

"THE SWORD AND THE STONED"

Aladdin and Jasmine chose not to get back together. It was a mutual decision, but as the genie said, "In a breakup there's always only one person who really walks away."

Aladdin sat in his window looking at the palace lit up above the city, and of course he thought of the old lamp. Everything he'd dreamed of had been possible for a brief moment. If he had known then what he knew now, what would he have wished for?

A generous heart and the love of someone with the same. Nothing else mattered.

As a joke, Puss in Boots started an
Etsy for "elegant evening wear for
cats," and by morning he'd already
gotten thousands of orders.

Jack was eventually stripped of his giant-killing medals when he was proven guilty of doping.

𝓐 lice woke up, hungover, at the foot of the Caterpillar's mushroom.

"You've changed," said the Caterpillar. "You are less sure of yourself than the last time you were here."

Alice knew he was right. Life got more confusing with each year, and there was no prescribed path for what to do next. How was she supposed to move forward?

When she looked up, the Caterpillar was gone. He'd become something new and was flying away.

The Tortoise and the Hare decided to meet for coffee.

They took turns casually mentioning their recent successes. The Hare was named one of the up-and-coming tech whizzes to watch. The Tortoise was coming out with a book of drawings he'd made in the margins of other people's poems.

"How original," the Hare commented.

They parted ways with a smile, the Hare hailing a cab and the Tortoise stretching his legs for a walk across the bridge.

It wasn't until they were each about to fall asleep that night that it hit them at the same time: There is no destination. There isn't a winner. There never was a race.

Peter Pan's first few days off the Internet were weird: Was there anyone out there approving of what he was doing at this very moment? And how was he supposed to know if something he said was clever if no one retweeted him?

But after that it was like all of his five senses became heightened as the noise in his head disappeared. He was waking back up to his life.

And he didn't even want to blog about it. He just wanted to breathe it in and be there for it.

As her gallery opening ended, Cinderella caught a glimpse of herself in the mirror and did a double take: She looked like the woman she'd wished she would become.

Her doubts and uncertainties lingered, they did, but she knew now they would never fully go away. They weren't a sign she was doing something wrong. Neither were her mistakes. Everything she'd been through, it was all just part of the story.